Little, Brown and Company

Time Warner Book Group
1271 Avenue of the Americas, New York, NY 10020
Visit our Web site at www.lb-kids.com

Printed in the United States of America          COM-UNI
                    First Edition: April 2006        10 9 8 7 6 5 4 3 2 1
ISBN 0-316-05774-6

# ARTHUR
## and the Dog Show

by Marc Brown

**LITTLE, BROWN AND COMPANY**
New York ∙ Boston

"Look, Pal!" said Arthur. "There's going to be a dog show on Saturday. We should enter. Maybe we'll win a prize."

Arthur took Pal out to the backyard. "If we want to do well, we have to practice. So, roll over, Pal."
Pal wagged his tail.
"Roll over!" Arthur said again.

Pal wagged his tail harder.

"Maybe we should start with something easier," said Arthur." Sit, Pal!"

Pal began digging a hole.

"No, no," said Arthur. "Like this."
Pal ran around him in circles.
"This will be harder than I thought," Arthur said.
"We need to practice."

Every day they practiced

and practiced

and practiced.

On the day of the show, Arthur got up early.
He gave Pal a bath and a good brushing.
"You need to look your best in the winner's circle," he explained.

There were lots of dogs at the dog show.
Some of them were all dressed up.
"Don't worry, Pal," said Arthur. "We'll show them."

DOG SHOW
REGISTRATION

When it was Arthur's turn, he led Pal into the ring.
"Sit, Pal," he said.
Pal rolled over.

"Wag your tail, Pal!" Arthur ordered.
Pal stood up on his back legs.
The judges did not look pleased.

At the end, Arthur didn't even look at Pal's score.
"It can't be good," he said. "All that work for nothing."

Pal came over and sniffed at Arthur, but Arthur didn't move.
So Pal began licking Arthur's face.
"Stop that, Pal. It tickles."
But Pal didn't stop. He kept licking and licking until Arthur
started to smile.

"You're right," Arthur said. "It's not the end of the world.
Come on, let's go home."
Arthur started to leave, but the judges stopped him.

And then they declared Pal a winner!